Oxford University Press, Walton Street, Oxford OX2 6DP
Oxford New York Toronto
Delhi Bombay Calcutta Madras Karachi
Petaling Jaya Singapore Hong Kong Tokyo
Nairobi Dar es Salaam Cape Town
Melbourne Auckland

and associated companies in
Beirut Berlin Ibadan Nicosia

*Oxford* is a trade mark of Oxford University Press


First published 1987

*British Library Cataloguing in Publication Data*
Englander, Alice
Magic ride.
I. Title
823'.914[J] PZ7

ISBN 0 19 279864 2

Typeset by PGT Graphic Design, Oxford
Printed in Hong Kong

# MAGIC RIDE

Alice Englander

Oxford University Press
Oxford Toronto Melbourne

Saturday evening at last! Tom had been looking forward to it all week. Mum and Dad had promised to take him to the fair.

They threaded their way through the jostling crowd. Diesel fumes mingled with the smell of fried onions. Music blared from loudspeakers over the racketing noise of the engines.

'Please can I go for a ride?' asked Tom.
Mum gave him some money. 'Keep in sight,' she said.
'We'll wait for you here, be back in ten minutes,' called his Dad.

Excited and a bit scared, Tom ran off towards the swings and the roundabouts.

'Hi, Tom!' Some of his friends called to him. Three of them were tightly squeezed into the seat of a swing. 'There's no room for you,' they squealed as they swept round, up and away into the twinkling sky.

Tom watched for a moment, then ran over to the dodgems.

'You can't drive on your own sonny,' said the man with the tickets. 'You're too young.'

Tom saw a big boy climb into a car on his own. 'Can I ride with you?' Tom asked.

'No, you're too little,' the boy said, and roared off.

Disappointed Tom wished he was bigger as he walked away.

He stopped in front of a carousel.

'Take a ride on the Golden Gallopers,' called the showman. He gave Tom a friendly wink. 'Little ones, half-price!'

At last Tom had found a ride. He climbed onto the carousel and chose a horse called Terry.

Suddenly the painted horse turned his head:
'Want to ride in a race?' he asked.

'I need a rider for the Golden Gallopers' Grand National Stakes.'

'Your Mum and Dad won't miss you, because today is June the thirty-first – a magic day for magic people.'

'But I'm not magic,' protested Tom.

'You will be if you ride with me. Come on.' Tom climbed into the saddle. 'Start the carousel!' Terry shouted to the showman, 'I've found a rider for the big race,' and they disappeared into a cloud of steam.

They arrived in no time at all . . .

They had come to Golden Gallopers' Racecourse where the crowds had gathered for the event of the year: the Golden Galloper's Grand National Stakes. People spilled out of the grandstand onto the terraces to place their bets.

Then the loudspeaker crackled: 'Will the runners and riders please assemble in the parade ring.'

'Whew! Only just in time,' said Terry, as they joined the other competitors.

Terry greeted old friends and rivals. Pretzel was there with his rider, the Count von Pumpernickel: Fi-Fi, the French filly, was being ridden by Monsieur Fou-Fou, who kept twirling his moustache. The Galloping Major had curly whiskers and waved his wooden leg. He was riding Haydock, a hunter from Huntingdon.

Donna Lasagne was riding side-saddle on Cannelloni, the Continental Cockerel. The Red Knight was on Dagobert, the Dragon of Dortmund. Leo the Lion from Lucca was accompanied by Lulu, the bare-back dancer, and finally Shamus the Shirehorse with his jockey, Shaun Shinnanigans, greeted them.

A trumpet fanfare called them to the starting gate and the starter raised his flag.

'I've never ridden in a race before,' whispered Tom nervously.

Everyone held their breath as they waited.
Then the starter brought down his arm.

'We're off!' gasped Tom.

Poor Cannelloni was left at the post, but Donna Lasagne urged him on, and they soon caught up with the backmarkers.

Tom shut his eyes as they raced towards the first fence, but Terry took it comfortably in his stride. They galloped along Rollercoaster Ridge, past Organgrinder's Gap, hooves thudding on the turf.

There was a long roll of thunder, then a sudden flash of lightening. Raindrops began to fall, faster and faster. The going became dark and treacherous as they entered Tympany Thicket. Frightened, Tom held on tightly to Terry's neck until the storm passed.

As the sky cleared, the front runners began to draw away from the rest of the field.
Tom and Terry stayed with them as they came to the next fence.

Then disaster! Dagobert the Dragon collided with Leo the Lion. Luckily no-one was hurt. The Red Knight and Lulu, Dagobert and Leo picked themselves up and watched as the others disappeared into the distance.

Next came Glockenspiel Creek, the water jump. Haydock the hunter was over first, but stumbled on landing. Fi-Fi didn't quite make it and splashed Monsieur Fou-Fou. But Pretzel and the Count jumped clear and Tom and Terry sailed over in style.

Tom looked back. Cannelloni had fallen head first into the water, and Donna Lasagne was soaking wet. She managed to get him going again.

Shamus was laughing so much at this sight, he had to go back and take the jump again.

'Hold tight,' said Terry. 'We're coming to the biggest fence in the race.'

Tom felt Terry tense himself for a supreme effort. A bold, magnificent jump landed them right up with the leaders.

The commentator's voice rose above the roaring race-goers. 'Here they come into the final furlong. Fi-Fi leads Pretzel by half-a-length, closely followed by Haydock. Good heavens, Cannelloni is making a comeback, but his challenge is too late. Tom and Terry are making up ground. It's anybody's race.'

'Hold tight!' cried Terry, 'the winning-post is in sight.'

Tom felt Terry tense himself for a supreme effort and with a magnificent burst of speed, raced right up to the leaders.

What a battle for first place! But at the post, by a neck, by a nose, by a whisker – it's Tom and Terry.'

The crowd went wild with excitement. Tom and Terry made their way back to the winner's enclosure. They were each presented with a blue rosette and celebrated their victory with ice-cream and candy floss.

'Listen Tom!' Terry said suddenly.

They heard the sound of familiar music above the merrymaking.

'It's the carousel – we must go – goodbye, goodbye everyone!'

In no time at all, Tom was back at the fair. 'Thanks Terry.' Tom gave him an affectionate hug and dismounted. Terry circled away on his barley-sugar pole.

Tom gave one last wave and ran back to his Mum and Dad. He wondered if he would ever tell them about his magic ride.